KEVIN D. CARATIQUIT, PhD
Author

GUARDIANS OF THE DIGITAL GALAXY

Cybersecurity for Beginners

GUARDIANS OF THE DIGITAL GALAXY: CYBERSECURITY FOR BEGINNERS

KEVIN D. CARATIQUIT, PhD
Senior High School Teacher III
Lal-lo National High School
Division of Cagayan
Author

Published by

Poetry Planet Book Publishing House

DEDICAT

To my cherished famil
have been the foundat
learners and readers, m
illuminating your path.
voyage, your camaraderi
to the Divine, the guidin
book as an expression of
that light our way in the v

COPYRIGHT PAGE

Guardians of the Digital Galaxy: Cybersecurity for Beginners

Softbound/Paperback: ISBN
Hardbound: ISBN
MOBI/KINDLE: ISBN

Published by

Poetry Planet Book Publishing House

Call or Text: 09554960044
Email: maritesritumalta@gmail.com | lovelypoetess95@gmail.com
Website: https://poetryplanet114433.wixsite.com/website-1

Registered with and Accredited by
the ***National Book Development Board of the Philippines***

ABOU

He is a Senior Higl
statistics subjects ir
his knowledge and
dedicated career rev
promoting academic
With a Doctor of P
Management, a Mas
Cagayan State Univ
Computer Science fr
commitment to perso

Moreover, he holds tl
Research and ICT
actively contribute
development. His
contributions, includin
articles published i
underscore his comi
progress. His research
and Learning, Comp
Educational Technol
dedication to enhancin
and effectively integ
education. His multifa
field of education and hi
aligns perfectly with the
provides in the book "**Gu**
Galaxy: Cybersecurity fo

KEVIN D. CARATIQU
Author

TABLE OF CONTENTS

FOREWORD

As the IT Officer of the Division of Cagayan, I am privileged to introduce **"Guardians of the Digital Galaxy: Cybersecurity for Beginners."** In today's interconnected world, the digital landscape is integral to education, communication, and everyday life. While this digital realm offers countless opportunities, it presents challenges, particularly cybersecurity. This book, authored by Kevin D. Caratiquit, a dedicated educator, provides a comprehensive roadmap for individuals navigating the digital cosmos.

This book equips readers with the essential knowledge and skills to ensure a safe and secure online experience. As our lives become increasingly intertwined with the digital galaxy, it is imperative to understand the cyber threats that lurk and the measures we can take to protect our digital starships. Mr. Caratiquit's expertise, commitment to academic advancement, and extensive experience make him an ideal guide in this journey toward digital security. I encourage everyone, from beginners to seasoned tech enthusiasts, to delve into this invaluable resource and become vigilant Guardians of the Digital Galaxy.

ANDREW TORIBIO B. TAACA, MIT, MPA, CHRA
Information Technology Officer I
Division of Cagayan

ACKNOWLEDGMENTS

Creating "**Guardians of the Digital Galaxy: Cybersecurity for Beginners"** has been a collective effort, and many individuals and resources have contributed to its existence. I would like to extend my gratitude to those who have played a significant role in bringing this book to fruition.

First and foremost, I thank the readers, for it is your curiosity, enthusiasm, and desire to enhance your cybersecurity knowledge that inspired me to create this guide. Your quest for digital security is at the heart of this book.

I also acknowledge the tireless efforts of the cybersecurity community and experts whose knowledge and insights have shaped the content within these pages. Also, I appreciate my family and friends who supported me throughout the writing process; your encouragement and understanding were invaluable as I embarked on this journey into the digital cosmos.

Lastly, I want to thank the team at the publishing house and the countless individuals who worked behind the scenes to bring this book to life. Your dedication to my vision is greatly appreciated.

As a Guardian of the Digital Galaxy, my mission is to promote digital safety and security for all. This book is a testament to my commitment, and I am grateful for the opportunity to share my knowledge and insights with you. Together, we will continue to explore the digital cosmos with confidence and resilience.

- Kevin D. Caratiquit, PhD

PREFACE

In the digital age, our lives are intrinsically intertwined with the vast expanse of the digital cosmos. This book, **"Guardians of the Digital Galaxy: Cybersecurity for Beginners,"** serves as your guiding light in this intricate digital universe. It is designed for individuals new to the digital realm and those seeking to reinforce their online security knowledge. Our goal is to provide you with the knowledge and skills required to navigate the digital cosmos securely and with confidence.

As you journey through the pages of this book, you will delve into the multifaceted landscape of the digital realm. The author aims to empower you to be a responsible guardian in the digital galaxy, capable of defending your digital starship against the lurking perils of the virtual cosmos.

The digital cosmos is vast and ever-evolving, and your expedition commences within these pages. The author invites you to explore the knowledge contained in this book, arm yourself with the tools to safeguard your digital world, and embrace your role as a Guardian of the Digital Galaxy. The digital universe awaits, and you are ready to navigate it with assurance and security.

- Kevin D. Caratiquit, PhD

Chapter 1

THE DIGITAL FRONTIER

Welcome to the digital frontier, a vast and ever-expanding landscape that has become an integral part of our daily lives. In this digital realm, we connect with friends and family, access information, conduct business, and engage in a myriad of activities that have reshaped the way we live, work, and play. Our smartphones, laptops, and other digital devices have become constant companions, providing us with the means to navigate this dynamic and interconnected world.

However, as we explore this frontier and embrace the conveniences and opportunities it offers, we must also confront the challenges it presents. The digital frontier is not without its perils. It's a realm where your personal information is stored, where your online identity is created and shared, and where your financial transactions take place. It's a place where your privacy and security are at risk.

1.1. Understanding the Digital Landscape

The digital landscape is a vast and intricate realm where our online lives unfold. It encompasses a multitude of digital spaces, technologies, and services that have transformed the way we communicate, work, shop, and entertain ourselves. To navigate this ever-evolving terrain effectively and make informed decisions about our digital security, it's crucial to have a fundamental understanding of the digital landscape.

The Digital Universe

Think of the digital landscape as a universe of information, interactions, and transactions that occur through the internet. It includes websites, mobile apps, social media platforms, email services, cloud storage, and more. This universe is teeming with content, connections, and data, making it an integral part of our modern existence.

Interconnectedness

The digital landscape's defining trait is its interconnectedness. Devices, services, and users are all linked together. This enables data transfer, global access to information, and interactions.

Digital Ecosystems

Within the digital landscape, various ecosystems exist. These ecosystems include the operating systems that power your devices (e.g., Android, iOS, Windows), software applications (e.g., Microsoft Office, Adobe Photoshop), and online platforms (e.g., Google, Facebook). Each ecosystem has its own set of rules, interfaces, and security considerations, which you will need to be aware of to navigate effectively.

The Expansion of the Cloud

The cloud is an essential part of the digital landscape. It refers to the storage and processing of data and applications on remote servers accessible through the Internet. Cloud services enable you to store files, run software, and access your data from anywhere. While convenient, it also introduces security considerations, as your data is no longer solely on your local device.

Digital Transformation

The digital landscape continually evolves, driven by technological advancements, innovation, and changing user behaviors. The way we shop, learn, work, and entertain ourselves has shifted due to this ongoing transformation. This evolution brings new opportunities and conveniences, but it also introduces new security challenges that must be addressed.

Significance of Digital Landscape Literacy

To effectively protect yourself and your digital assets, it's essential to comprehend the digital landscape and its intricacies. Without this understanding, you may unknowingly put your privacy and security at risk. Here are a few reasons why understanding the digital landscape is vital:

1. **Informed Decision-Making.** When you understand the digital landscape, you can make informed decisions about the technology and services you use, choosing those that align with your privacy and security preferences.

2. **Threat Awareness.** Recognizing the elements of the digital landscape helps you identify potential threats and vulnerabilities that cybercriminals may exploit.

3. **Cybersecurity Practices.** An understanding of the digital landscape is the foundation for implementing effective cybersecurity practices. It allows you to tailor your security measures to the specific risks you encounter.

4. **Privacy Protection.** Being aware of how your data is collected, used, and stored online empowers you to take steps to protect your privacy.

As we delve into the digital landscape, we'll explore different digital spaces, their underlying technologies, and the related security concerns. This knowledge will help you navigate the digital world with confidence and security.

1.2. The Importance of Cybersecurity

In this section, we delve into a critical topic that affects everyone in this digital age: cybersecurity. Cybersecurity is safeguarding your digital presence, information, and assets from the countless threats that exist in the digital realm. It's a subject that goes beyond the realm of IT professionals and security experts; it's a matter that concerns every individual who ventures into the digital frontier.

But why is cybersecurity so critical? The answer lies in the consequences of neglecting it. In an interconnected world, cyberattacks and data breaches have become common, resulting in devastating consequences for individuals, businesses, and governments. These breaches can lead to financial losses, identity theft, privacy invasions, and the compromise of sensitive information.

Understanding and practicing cybersecurity is essential to protect yourself and your digital assets from these threats. A digital frontier is a place of both wonder and danger. By the end of this chapter, you will have a clear understanding of why you should care about cybersecurity and the role you play as a guardian of your digital galaxy. This chapter is your first step in building the knowledge and skills to navigate this frontier confidently and securely.

In an age where the digital world plays an increasingly central role in our lives, the importance of cybersecurity cannot be overstated. It has become an indispensable part of our modern existence, and understanding why it matters is the first step toward safeguarding your digital presence and assets.

The Digital Threat Landscape

The digital frontier is fraught with threats and dangers that can affect anyone who ventures into this realm. These threats are not limited to a specific group or category; they target individuals, businesses, and governments. To truly appreciate the importance of cybersecurity, it's essential to understand the nature of these threats.

1. Malware and Viruses. Malware, short for malicious software, is a broad category that includes viruses, Trojans, spyware, and ransomware, among others. These malicious programs are designed to infiltrate your devices and systems, often to steal data, damage your digital assets, or extort money.

2. Phishing Attacks. Phishing attacks are a common and insidious threat in the digital world. They involve deceptive emails, messages, or websites that mimic legitimate sources to trick individuals into revealing sensitive information such as passwords, credit card numbers, or personal data.

3. Identity Theft. Identity theft is the fraudulent acquisition and use of someone's personal information, typically for financial gain. In the digital realm, identity theft can have severe consequences, including financial loss and reputational damage.

4. Privacy Invasion. The digital world is replete with opportunities for privacy invasion. Hackers and cybercriminals can gain unauthorized access to your personal data, compromising your privacy and potentially exploiting it for nefarious purposes.

5. Financial Loss. Cyberattacks can lead to significant financial losses, not only for individuals but also for businesses. These losses may result from theft, fraud, or damage to digital assets.

6. Disruption of Services. In some cases, cyberattacks can disrupt essential services, affecting not only individuals but also critical infrastructure and businesses, leading to widespread chaos.

The Universal Concern

The importance of cybersecurity transcends age, profession, or technical expertise. It is a universal concern because, in today's interconnected world, virtually everyone is a digital citizen. Whether you're a student, a professional, a parent, or a retiree, you have a presence in the digital frontier. Your digital realm is a repository of personal information, memories, and potentially valuable assets.

Neglecting cybersecurity is not an option. It's a responsibility that comes with our participation in the digital world. It's about protecting what matters to you, be it your personal information, your financial well-being, or your online identity.

As we progress through this book, you will learn the fundamental concepts and practical strategies necessary to safeguard your digital presence effectively. The digital galaxy is vast and full of wonders, but it's also filled with risks. By understanding the importance of cybersecurity, you are taking the first step toward becoming a guardian of your digital realm.

1.3. The Guardian's Role in the Digital Galaxy

In the vast and dynamic expanse of the digital galaxy, each of us plays a vital role as a guardian. Our digital lives, whether for personal, professional, or recreational purposes, are increasingly interconnected, and with this interconnectivity comes the responsibility to protect what matters most to us. This chapter explores your role as a guardian of the digital galaxy and the significance of actively participating in safeguarding your digital realm.

Your Digital Frontier

Your digital frontier is the space where your online activities and interactions take place. It encompasses social media profiles, email accounts, online banking, e-commerce transactions, and much more. It's the space where you share your thoughts, store your memories, and conduct various aspects of your life. Just as you would protect your physical home, it's equally important to protect your digital space.

Embracing the Role of Guardian

As a digital citizen, you are entrusted with the task of safeguarding your digital presence and the information that resides within it. Here's why your role as a guardian is so crucial:

1. Personal Security. Your online identity is an extension of your physical self, and its security is paramount. Protecting it ensures that you are shielded from identity theft, financial loss, and privacy breaches.

2. Protection of Assets. Your digital assets, such as photographs, documents, and even financial records, are stored in the digital realm. Being a guardian means ensuring the safety of these assets.

3. Cyber Hygiene. Good digital practices and security measures not only protect you but also contribute to the overall health of the digital galaxy. The more individuals practice cybersecurity, the more challenging it becomes for cybercriminals to exploit vulnerabilities.

4. Community Well-being. Your actions in the digital galaxy affect not only you but also your community. By practicing good cybersecurity, you contribute to the collective security of the digital frontier.

Guardianship in Action

Being a guardian in the digital galaxy involves taking proactive steps to protect yourself and your online presence. This includes:

1. **Educating Yourself.** Understanding the threats and vulnerabilities in the digital realm is the first step toward being an effective guardian.

2. **Adopting Best Practices.** Implementing strong password management, being cautious online, and keeping your software current are essential practices.

3. **Sharing Knowledge.** As you learn about cybersecurity, you can help educate your friends, family, and community, creating a safer digital environment for everyone.

4. **Using Security Tools.** Leveraging cybersecurity tools such as antivirus software, firewalls, and encryption can significantly enhance your defenses.

5. **Remaining Vigilant.** Awareness of potential threats and staying vigilant in digital activities is a cornerstone of guardianship.

Your role as a guardian in the digital galaxy is a responsibility that extends to all corners of the digital world. By taking this role seriously, you contribute to a safer and more secure online environment, not just for yourself but for the digital community.

Chapter 2

THE THREATS BEYOND

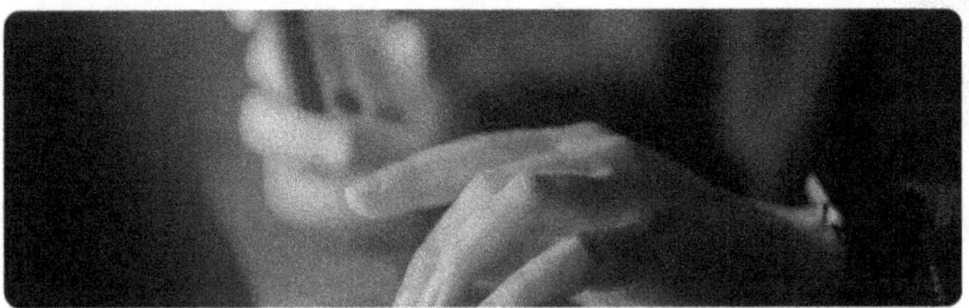

As we continue our journey through the digital galaxy, we must confront the hidden perils that await us in the shadows. "The Threats Beyond" is a chapter dedicated to unveiling the darker side of our digital realm. Within these virtual expanses, insidious threats such as phishing attacks and malware hide, ready to compromise our online security and privacy. By understanding and identifying these digital adversaries, you'll be better equipped to navigate the digital world with a heightened awareness and the tools to protect your online presence.

The digital frontier, like any other vast territory, presents both opportunities and dangers. In this chapter, we highlight the threats that lie beyond the surface, helping you develop the skills and knowledge needed to defend against them. By the end of this exploration, you'll be better prepared to safeguard your digital existence from the perils that lurk in the shadows, ensuring a safer and more secure digital journey.

2.1. Identifying Common Cybersecurity Threats

In the digital landscape, being able to recognize and understand common cybersecurity threats is a fundamental skill for anyone navigating the digital galaxy. These threats come in various forms, each with its tactics and objectives. By learning to identify these threats, you empower yourself to take proactive measures to safeguard your digital presence and assets. In this section, we will explore some of the most prevalent cybersecurity threats that individuals and organizations encounter:

1. **Phishing Attacks.** Phishing is a common tactic where cybercriminals use deceit to trick individuals into revealing sensitive data, like usernames and passwords. They often employ fraudulent emails or websites that mimic trusted entities. Recognizing phishing is crucial as it can lead to identity theft and financial loss.

2. **Malware.** Malware is a broad category of malicious software, including viruses, Trojans, spyware, and ransomware. It can infiltrate your devices, corrupt files, and steal data. Typically, it's spread through infected downloads, email attachments or compromised websites. Detecting malware signs and implementing security measures are essential for digital safety.

3. Social Engineering. Social engineering attacks manipulate human psychology to deceive individuals into revealing confidential information. These tactics exploit trust, fear, or urgency. Common examples include pretexting (creating a fabricated scenario to obtain information) and baiting (enticing individuals to click on malicious links or download infected files). Learning to recognize these manipulative techniques is crucial in thwarting social engineering threats.

4. Insider Threats. Not all cybersecurity threats come from external sources. Insider threats originate within an organization, often involving employees or contractors who misuse their access to compromise security. Detecting suspicious behavior and implementing robust access controls can help mitigate the risks associated with insider threats.

5. DDoS Attacks. Distributed Denial of Service (DDoS) attacks flood a network or website with an overwhelming amount of traffic, rendering it inaccessible to legitimate users. Recognizing the signs of a DDoS attack and having contingency plans to mitigate its effects is critical for businesses and individuals who rely on online services.

6. Zero-Day Vulnerabilities. Zero-day vulnerabilities are software flaws or weaknesses exploited by attackers before the software developers have had a chance to create patches or updates. Staying informed about the latest security updates and adopting best practices to minimize the impact of zero-day vulnerabilities is essential.

7. Eavesdropping and Man-in-the-Middle Attacks.

Eavesdropping attacks involve intercepting and monitoring communication between two parties without their knowledge. Man-in-the-middle attacks occur when an attacker intercepts and possibly alters the communication between two parties. Recognizing signs of compromised communication channels is crucial to protect sensitive data.

By becoming familiar with these common cybersecurity threats, you're better equipped to identify them and take the necessary steps to protect yourself and your digital assets. Vigilance, knowledge, and proactive cybersecurity measures are your most potent tools against these threats in the ever-evolving digital frontier.

2.2. Malware, Phishing, and Social Engineering

In the realm of cybersecurity, three primary threats consistently make headlines and pose significant risks to individuals and organizations: malware, phishing, and social engineering. Understanding these threats is vital to your digital security.

Malware: The Silent Intruder

Malware, a fusion of the words "malicious" and "software," is a broad term encompassing various forms of harmful software designed to infiltrate your devices, corrupt your files, or steal your data. Malware includes viruses, Trojans, spyware, ransomware, and more.

1. Viruses. These self-replicating programs attach themselves to legitimate files and infect other files on your device. Viruses can damage files and render your system unstable.

2. Trojans. Named after the legendary Trojan Horse, Trojans disguise themselves as legitimate software, enticing users to install them. Once inside, they can provide cybercriminals with unauthorized access to your device.

3. Spyware. As the name suggests, spyware secretly monitors your activities, collecting data such as login credentials, financial information, and browsing habits. It then transmits this information to a remote server.

4. Ransomware. This malicious software encrypts your files, rendering them inaccessible. Cybercriminals demand a ransom to provide the decryption key, although paying doesn't guarantee you'll regain access.

Preventing malware involves using reputable antivirus software, avoiding suspicious downloads, keeping your software up to date, and practicing safe browsing habits.

Phishing: The Deceptive Lure

Phishing attacks are notorious for their deceptive tactics. Cybercriminals create fake emails, messages, or websites that appear to come from trusted entities. They aim to trick you into revealing sensitive information, such as usernames, passwords, and financial data. Phishing attacks can lead to identity theft, financial loss, and unauthorized account access.

Recognizing phishing attempts is crucial. Please pay attention to suspicious email addresses, check for misspellings or irregular URLs, and be careful when asked for sensitive information. Always verify the authenticity of requests, especially if they seem urgent or unusual.

Social Engineering: The Manipulative Art

Social engineering is the art of manipulating individuals into revealing confidential information or performing actions that compromise security. This attack relies on psychology and human interaction to deceive individuals. Common techniques include pretexting (creating a fabricated scenario to obtain information) and baiting (enticing individuals to click on malicious links or download infected files).

Defending against social engineering involves skepticism, verifying the identities of those requesting information, and maintaining confidentiality regarding personal and financial data. Education and awareness are essential, as individuals who understand the tactics are less likely to fall victim to social engineering attacks.

In the digital galaxy, understanding malware, phishing, and social engineering is your first line of defense. By recognizing these threats and implementing effective security measures, you can navigate the digital world with greater confidence and resilience, protecting your digital realm from shadowy dangers beyond the surface.

2.3. The Dark Side of the Internet

While the Internet offers a wealth of information, convenience, and opportunities, it also has a dark side, harboring various threats and illicit activities. Understanding this darker aspect of the digital realm is essential for ensuring your safety and security in the online world.

Cybercrime and Illicit Activities

The dark side of the internet encompasses a range of cybercriminal activities. These include:

1. Hacking and Data Breaches. Exploiting system vulnerabilities for unauthorized access, potentially leading to data breaches.

2. Identity Theft. Stealing personal data for fraudulent use.

3. Online Fraud. Various online scams and schemes, from investment fraud to shopping scams.

4. Child Exploitation. Criminal activities involving child exploitation, including explicit content sharing and grooming.

5. Dark Web. The dark web, a hidden part of the internet, hosts illicit marketplaces for drugs, weapons, and stolen data. It also serves as a hub for illegal activities, including hacking services for hire.

Malicious Software and Cyber Threats

Malicious software, such as viruses, Trojans, and ransomware, is prevalent on the dark side of the internet. Cybercriminals use these tools to infiltrate devices, steal data, and demand ransoms. Additionally, Distributed Denial of Service (DDoS) attacks, which flood websites or networks with traffic to render them inaccessible, are often launched from this hidden territory.

Protecting Yourself from the Dark Side

To safeguard your digital presence from the dark side of the internet, follow these fundamental practices:

1. Stay Informed. Keep up-to-date with the latest cybersecurity threats and scams. Understanding these dangers is the first step toward protecting yourself.

2. Use Strong Authentication. Implement strong, unique passwords and enable two-factor authentication for your accounts.

3. Avoid Suspicious Websites. Be cautious about the websites you visit, downloads you make, and links you click. Stick to reputable sources.

4. Security Software. Install and regularly update antivirus and anti-malware software to protect your devices.
Privacy Measures: Protect your personal information by limiting what you share online and being cautious about revealing sensitive data.

5. Educate Others. Share your knowledge about online safety with friends and family, helping them stay safe.

Understanding the dark side of the internet is crucial for making informed decisions in the digital world. By staying vigilant and practicing good cybersecurity habits, you can better protect yourself from the threats that lurk in the shadowy corners of the online realm.

Chapter 3

THE ARMOR OF THE GUARDIAN

In the vast digital galaxy, every guardian must have the proper armor to protect their digital realm. This chapter, aptly titled "The Armor of the Guardian," explores the essential tools, practices, and strategies that fortify your defenses against many threats in the digital frontier. Just as a knight wouldn't venture into battle without armor, a digital guardian must have the knowledge and skills to safeguard their online presence.

We will uncover the indispensable components of digital armor, from strong and secure passwords to encryption, antivirus software, and best practices for maintaining the security of your devices and accounts. As we journey through this chapter, you will acquire the know-how to fortify your digital defenses, creating a formidable barrier between you and the threats that loom in the digital world. So, wear your digital armor and prepare to emerge from this chapter with a heightened sense of security and resilience in the face of digital adversaries.

3.1. Creating Strong and Secure Passwords

Passwords are the digital keys to your online realm, guarding access to your personal information, financial accounts, and digital assets. To ensure the utmost security, creating strong and secure passwords is the first line of defense against cyber threats. This section delves into the art and science of password creation, providing you with the knowledge and techniques necessary to fortify your digital armor.

The Importance of Strong Passwords

Passwords serve as the initial gatekeepers to your digital life, making it imperative to understand their significance. Weak or easily guessable passwords are related to leaving your front door unlocked in the real world. Cybercriminals can exploit these vulnerabilities to compromise your accounts, steal your personal information, and wreak havoc on your digital existence.

Characteristics of Strong Passwords

Strong passwords are vital characteristics that make them difficult for cybercriminals to crack. They typically include:

1. Length. Longer passwords are generally more secure. A good rule of thumb is to aim for at least 12 characters.

2. Complexity. A strong password includes uppercase and lowercase letters, numbers, and special characters.

3. Unpredictability. Avoid using easily guessable information like birthdays, common phrases, or names.

4. Uniqueness. Each account should have a unique password. Reusing passwords across multiple accounts increases your vulnerability if one account is compromised.

Creating Strong Passwords

Crafting strong passwords doesn't need to be an onerous task. You can employ several strategies to make the process more manageable:

1. Passphrases. Consider creating a passphrase by stringing together multiple random words. Passphrases are easier to remember and more secure.

2. Random Combinations. Generate a password using a random combination of characters, including letters, numbers, and symbols.

3. Avoid Dictionary Words. Refrain from using complete words or phrases that can be found in dictionaries.

4. Long but Memorable. Opt for a lengthy password that is still memorable, such as a combination of words and numbers.

5. Password Managers. Password management tools can generate, store, and auto-fill complex passwords for you, alleviating the need to remember them all.

Regular Password Updates

In addition to creating strong passwords, it's essential to update them regularly. Frequent password changes can help thwart potential threats. Remember, though, that the most secure passwords are of little use if they are compromised due to poor handling. Safeguard your passwords, don't share them unnecessarily, and store them securely.

By understanding the importance of strong passwords and employing the techniques outlined here, you can significantly enhance your digital security. Your strong and secure passwords are the first layer of your digital armor, and they play a pivotal role in protecting your digital realm from unwanted intrusions and safeguarding your online presence.

3.2. Two-Factor Authentication and Biometrics

In an age where digital security is paramount, using traditional usernames and passwords alone is no longer sufficient to protect our online accounts and sensitive information. Cybercriminals continually develop sophisticated methods to breach these barriers. As a result, the need for enhanced authentication measures has become crucial. Two-factor authentication (2FA) and biometrics offer potent solutions to bolster digital security.

Two-factor authentication (2FA)

Two-factor authentication, or 2FA, adds an extra layer of security beyond a username and password. It typically involves something you know (your password) and something you have (a second authentication method). This secondary method can take various forms, including:

1. Text Messages or Email Codes: You receive a one-time code via text message or email, which you must enter after your password to access your account. This code changes with every login attempt, enhancing security.

2. Authentication Apps: Mobile apps like Google Authenticator or Authy generate time-sensitive codes you enter during login.

3. Biometric Verification. Biometric data, such as fingerprints or facial recognition, is the second factor in accessing your accounts.

4. Hardware Tokens. Physical devices, like security keys, generate unique codes when plugged into your computer or mobile device.

2FA significantly enhances security because even if someone obtains your password, they won't be able to access your account without the second authentication factor. This makes it considerably more challenging for cybercriminals to breach your bills, and it's a recommended security practice for all your critical online services.

Biometrics: The Human Touch

Biometrics involves using unique physical or behavioral characteristics to verify your identity. These characteristics include fingerprints, facial features, retina or iris scans, voice recognition, and behavioral patterns like keystroke dynamics. Biometric authentication is appealing for several reasons:

1. Uniqueness. Each person's biometric data is distinct, making it incredibly difficult to impersonate.

2. Convenience. Using biometrics is often more convenient than remembering and entering passwords.

3. Security. It's challenging to fake or replicate biometric data, making it a robust security measure.

4. No Passwords to Remember. Biometrics eliminates the need to recall and enter passwords, which can be prone to theft or forgetting.

However, biometrics are only partially foolproof, as they can be subject to spoofing or hacking in some cases. Thus, combining biometrics with 2FA is an even more secure approach.

Two-Factor Authentication and biometrics represent essential tools in the guardian's arsenal to protect their digital realm. By implementing these security measures for your online accounts and devices, you significantly reduce the risk of unauthorized access and enhance the overall security of your digital presence.

3.3. Locking Down Your Devices

In an era where our personal and professional lives are increasingly entwined with technology, securing our digital devices is paramount. Whether it's a smartphone, tablet, laptop, or desktop computer, locking down your devices ensures that your data, privacy, and digital identity remain well-protected.

The Importance of Device Security

Our devices are repositories of personal and sensitive information, making them desirable targets for cybercriminals. Securing your devices is not just about protecting the physical device but also the data and accounts it connects to. Here are some of the critical reasons why device security matters:

1. **Data Privacy.** Your devices store a treasure trove of personal data, from photos and messages to financial information and emails. Keeping this data private and secure is essential.

2. **Online Accounts.** Your devices are gateways to your online accounts. A compromised device can lead to unauthorized access to your email, social media, banking, and other accounts.

3. **Digital Identity.** Securing your devices safeguards your digital identity, preventing identity theft and impersonation.

4. Peace of Mind: Knowing that your devices are well-protected brings peace of mind, enabling you to confidently use technology.

Key Steps for Device Security

Securing your devices involves implementing several key steps:

1. Strong and Unique Passcodes. Use strong, unique passcodes or PINs to lock your devices. Avoid easily guessable codes, and consider using biometrics like fingerprints or facial recognition if available.
2. Full Disk Encryption. Enable full disk encryption on your devices. This protects your data even if the device falls into the wrong hands.

3. Regular Updates. Keep your device's operating system and software up to date. Updates often include security patches to fix known vulnerabilities.

4. App Permissions. Review and manage app permissions. Only grant apps access to the data and features they genuinely need.

5. Install Security Software. Use reputable security software, such as antivirus and anti-malware, to protect your devices from threats.

6. Backup Your Data. Regularly back up your device's data to prevent data loss in case of theft or damage.

7. Secure Wi-Fi Connections. Avoid connecting to unsecured public Wi-Fi networks, and use a virtual private network (VPN) for added security when connecting to the internet.

8. Remote Wiping. Set up remote wipe capabilities, which allow you to erase your device's data if it's lost or stolen.

9. App Updates. Keep your apps updated, as outdated apps can contain security vulnerabilities.

10. Device Tracking. Use device tracking and location services to help locate your device in case it's lost or stolen.

Education and Vigilance

Security is not a one-time action but an ongoing practice. Educate yourself about the latest threats and security best practices. Stay vigilant and skeptical of suspicious messages or prompts on your devices. By maintaining a proactive approach to device security, you can enjoy the benefits of technology while safeguarding your digital presence. Locking down your devices is similar to locking the front door of your digital home, protecting your online world from unwelcome intrusions.

Chapter 4

NAVIGATING THE CYBER COSMOS

Welcome to "Navigating the Cyber Cosmos," a chapter that embarks on a journey into the intricate digital galaxy that now envelops our lives. In this age of interconnectedness and technological advancements, our online experiences have become an integral part of modern existence. This chapter sets the stage for exploring the digital landscapes and technological constellations that shape our digital universe.

Just as early explorers faced challenges, today's digital citizens encounter risks and rewards online. "Navigating the Cyber Cosmos" equips you with the skills to be a confident and secure traveler in this digital universe so you can navigate it with assurance and resilience.

4.1. Safe Browsing Practices

As the internet has become an integral part of our daily lives, practicing safe browsing has never been more critical. The web is a vast digital landscape, and while it offers a wealth of information, entertainment, and opportunities, it also presents numerous hazards. Cyber threats, malicious websites, and privacy concerns loom on the horizon. Adopting safe browsing practices is essential to protect your digital well-being and personal information.

The Importance of Safe Browsing

Safe browsing is not just about avoiding malicious websites; it's about safeguarding your data, privacy, and online security. Here are some of the key reasons why safe browsing practices are crucial:

1. **Protecting Personal Information.** Safeguarding sensitive information like your login credentials, financial data, and personal details is vital in the digital age. Safe browsing helps prevent this information from falling into the wrong hands.

2. **Preventing Malware.** Malicious websites and downloads can infect your devices with malware, leading to data loss, financial theft, and other digital nightmares.

3. Avoiding Scams and Phishing. Safe browsing practices help you steer clear of scams and phishing attempts that trick users into revealing personal and financial information.

4. Privacy Preservation. Protecting your online privacy is becoming increasingly important. Safe browsing practices help minimize tracking and data collection by advertisers and other third parties.

Key Safe Browsing Practices

1. Use Reputable Websites. Stick to well-known, reputable websites for your online activities, whether shopping, banking, or accessing information. Check for secure connections (look for "https://") when providing personal information.

2. Install Ad and Script Blockers. Ad and script blockers can help prevent malicious ads and scripts from running on your device, reducing the risk of malware infection.

3. Keep Software Updated. Ensure that your operating system, browser, and security software are updated with the latest security patches.

4. Exercise Caution with Email Links and Attachments. Be cautious when clicking on links or opening attachments in emails, especially if they are unexpected or seem suspicious.

5. Use Strong Passwords. Implement strong, unique passwords for your online accounts, and consider using a password manager to keep track of them.

6. Secure Wi-Fi Connections. Avoid using public Wi-Fi networks for sensitive activities like online banking. If you must use public Wi-Fi, consider using a virtual private network (VPN).

7. Educate Yourself. Stay informed about the latest online threats and scams. Awareness is your first line of defense.

8. Regular Backups. Keep regular data backups to prevent data loss in an unexpected incident.

Remember, the internet can be safe and rewarding when approached with vigilance and awareness. Practicing safe browsing habits will not only protect your digital well-being but also grant you the freedom to explore and enjoy the vast digital cosmos with confidence.

4.2. Safe Browsing Practices

In the digital age, your online identity extends your real-world self. It encompasses your personal information, digital presence, and activities on the internet. Protecting your online identity is crucial, as it safeguards your privacy, security, and reputation in the vast digital cosmos. As you navigate the online world, it's essential to take proactive steps to ensure the safety of your digital identity.

The Significance of Online Identity Protection

Your online identity is a multifaceted entity comprising your email accounts, social media profiles, online banking information, and more. Protecting it is of paramount importance for several key reasons:

1. Privacy. Preserving your privacy in the digital realm is a fundamental right. Your online identity contains personal data, and protecting it keeps your private information from being exploited or misused.

2. Security. A compromised online identity can lead to unauthorized access to your accounts, financial loss, or cyberattacks. Secure online identity practices help mitigate these risks.

3. Reputation. Your online activities can influence your reputation, both personally and professionally. Protecting your online identity ensures that you maintain control over how you are perceived in the digital world.

4. **Financial Safety.** Many of our online activities involve financial transactions, from online shopping to banking. Protecting your online identity is essential to prevent financial theft or fraud.

Key Steps to Protect Your Online Identity

1. Use Strong, Unique Passwords. Create strong and unique passwords for your online accounts. Avoid using the same password across multiple accounts.

2. Enable Two-Factor Authentication (2FA). Whenever possible, activate 2FA on your accounts. This additional layer of security makes it significantly harder for unauthorized users to gain access.

3. Beware of Phishing. Be cautious of phishing attempts, especially in emails or messages that request personal information or provide suspicious links. Verify the legitimacy of such requests.

4. Regularly Update Software. Keep your device's operating system and applications up to date to protect against vulnerabilities attackers could exploit.

5. Secure Wi-Fi Connections. Use secure, encrypted Wi-Fi connections, and avoid public Wi-Fi networks for sensitive activities.

6. Monitor Your Online Presence. Regularly review your online presence, including social media accounts and online profiles. Ensure that the information you share aligns with your desired online identity.

7. Educate Yourself. Stay informed about the latest online threats and scams, and educate yourself about privacy settings on various online platforms.

8. Use a Virtual Private Network (VPN). Consider using a VPN to encrypt your internet connection and enhance your online privacy.

Taking these steps will help you protect your online identity from the many threats that exist in the digital realm. By securing your online identity, you not only preserve your privacy and reputation but also enjoy a safer and more confident digital journey.

4.3. Recognizing and Avoiding Phishing Attacks

Phishing attacks are among the most prevalent and deceptive cyber threats in the digital landscape. These attacks use cunning and deceit to trick individuals into revealing sensitive information, such as usernames, passwords, financial data, and personal details. Recognizing and avoiding phishing attacks is a fundamental skill in safeguarding your online identity and security.

Understanding Phishing

Phishing attacks typically involve cybercriminals posing as trusted entities, often through email, messaging, or fraudulent websites. These attackers craft convincing messages, often employing psychological tactics to manipulate the recipient. Their primary goal is to persuade individuals to take specific actions that benefit the attacker, such as clicking on a malicious link or providing sensitive information.

Recognizing Phishing Attempts

Recognizing phishing attempts is the first line of defense against these deceptive attacks. Here are some key indicators of phishing:

1. Unsolicited Emails or Messages. Exercise caution when dealing with unsolicited emails or messages received from unknown senders or unfamiliar sources. These messages can serve as potential gateways for cyber threats, and clicking on links or opening attachments within them can lead to various cybersecurity risks.

2. Urgency or Fear Tactics. Phishing emails often use urgency or fear to push recipients into immediate action, such as claiming that an account will be closed unless you provide information.

3. Misspellings and Grammatical Errors. Many phishing messages contain spelling and grammatical mistakes, which are uncommon in official communications from legitimate organizations.

4. Suspicious Links. Hover your mouse pointer over email links to see where they lead before clicking. Be wary of URLs that don't match the legitimate domain of the organization.

5. Requests for Personal Information. Legitimate organizations rarely request sensitive information through email or messages. Be skeptical of any such requests.

6. Generic Greetings. Phishing messages may use generic greetings like "Dear Customer" instead of addressing you by name.

Avoiding Phishing Attacks

Once you recognize a potential phishing attempt, it's vital to take the following precautions:

1. Do Not Click on Suspicious Links. Avoid clicking on any links or downloading attachments in suspicious emails or messages.

2. Verify the Source. If you receive an email requesting information or actions, verify the source by contacting the organization through official channels before responding.

3. Use 2FA. Enable two-factor authentication (2FA) on your accounts to provide an extra layer of security even if your login credentials are compromised.

4. Educate Yourself and Others. Stay informed about the latest phishing techniques and educate your family, friends, and colleagues to recognize and avoid phishing attacks.

5. Report Phishing. Report phishing attempts to your email provider, the organization being impersonated, and relevant authorities.

In the complex web of our digitally interconnected world, recognizing and adeptly avoiding phishing attacks is the key to securing your online existence. By mastering these skills, you emerge as the sentry of your digital realm, shielding your online identity, safeguarding sensitive information, and fortifying your financial assets against the malevolent clutches of cybercriminals. Your shield is formed from layers of unwavering vigilance, a discerning eye for deception, and the knowledge you gather. This defense ensures that you stand firm, ready to face the deceptive forces that permeate the digital galaxy.

As you embrace your role as the guardian of your digital domain, remember that this ongoing battle against cyber deception demands your continuous vigilance and a healthy dose of skepticism. Your ever-deepening knowledge is the anchor of your resilience, enabling you to traverse the digital cosmos with the unwavering confidence that comes from mastering the art of recognizing and evading phishing attacks.

Chapter 5

DEFENDING YOUR DIGITAL STARSHIP

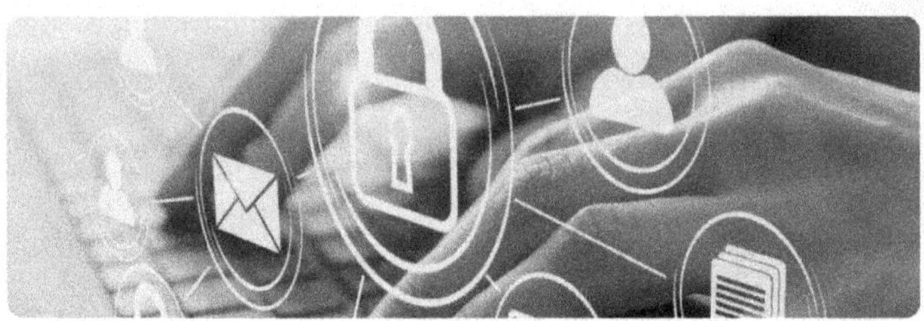

In the vast expanse of the digital cosmos, your devices and online presence serve as your very own starship, navigating the digital universe with you at the helm. However, like any spacefaring vessel, your digital starship faces various potential threats, from cyberattacks and malware to data breaches and privacy intrusions.

In the chapter "Defending Your Digital Starship," we guide you in strengthening your online security, similar to how historical explorers protected their vessels from dangers. This chapter covers tools, strategies, and practices to help you safeguard your digital journey and navigate the online world with confidence, just like spacefaring explorers did with preparation, vigilance, and knowledge.

5.1. Firewall and Antivirus Essentials

Firewalls and antivirus software are the digital sentinels that stand guard at the gates of your digital starship. These cybersecurity essentials serve as crucial components in the defense against the myriad threats in the digital cosmos. Understanding the role of firewalls and antivirus software and how to implement them effectively is paramount to ensuring the security of your digital journey.

The Firewall: Your Digital Fortress

A firewall acts as a digital fortress, shielding your devices and network from malicious intrusions. It functions as a barrier, filtering incoming and outgoing internet traffic to protect your digital starship from unauthorized access and cyber threats. Here's why firewalls are essential:

1. Traffic Filtering. Firewalls analyze network data packets and block any that don't adhere to your security rules, preventing potentially harmful traffic from reaching your devices.

2. Intrusion Detection and Prevention. Advanced firewalls include intrusion detection and prevention systems (IDPS) that identify and thwart unauthorized access and cyberattacks.

3. Protection Against Malware. Some firewalls offer malware filtering to block malicious content and downloads.

4. Network Privacy. Firewalls help safeguard your network's privacy by controlling the data that enters and exits.

The Role of Antivirus Software

Antivirus software is designed to detect, prevent, and remove malicious software (malware) from your devices. Malware includes viruses, Trojans, ransomware, spyware, and other malicious programs. The primary functions of antivirus software include:

1. Scanning for Malware. Antivirus software scans your device's files and system for known patterns and behaviors of malware.

2. Real-Time Protection. Many modern antivirus programs offer real-time protection, constantly monitoring your device for malware threats.

3. Removal of Threats. If malware is detected, the antivirus software quarantines or removes it, preventing harm to your device.

4. Regular Updates. Antivirus software requires regular updates to keep up with the evolving threat landscape.

Implementing Firewall and Antivirus Protection

1. Firewall Setup. Enable the built-in firewall on your router and configure it according to your security needs. Additionally, consider using a software firewall on your devices for an added layer of protection.

2. Antivirus Installation. Install reputable antivirus software on all your devices, including computers, smartphones, and tablets. Keep it up to date with the latest malware definitions and software updates.

3. Regular Scanning. Schedule regular antivirus scans of your devices to ensure that no hidden malware is lurking.

4. Educate Yourself. Understand how firewalls and antivirus software work and stay informed about potential threats and best practices in cybersecurity.

5. Automatic Updates. Enable automatic updates for your firewall and antivirus software to ensure they remain effective against emerging threats.

Firewalls and antivirus software are your steadfast companions on your digital voyage. When deployed effectively, they provide a formidable defense against the diverse threats that navigate the digital cosmos. By implementing these essentials, you fortify your digital starship, ensuring a secure and resilient journey in the digital universe.

5.2. Setting Up a Secure Wi-Fi Network

A secure Wi-Fi network is the foundation of your digital starship's defenses. In an era where our devices are interconnected and our online activities span from remote work and streaming to online shopping and communication, ensuring the security of your home network is paramount. Setting up a secure Wi-Fi network not only safeguards your data but also shields your digital realm from potential threats.

The Importance of Wi-Fi Security

Wi-Fi networks are convenient gateways to the digital cosmos, but they can also be vulnerable to intrusions and attacks if not properly secured. The significance of Wi-Fi security lies in the following key aspects:

1. **Data Protection.** A secure Wi-Fi network encrypts the data transmitted between your devices and the internet, safeguarding it from eavesdropping.

2. **Privacy Preservation.** A secure network helps protect your online privacy, preventing unauthorized access to your online activities and accounts.

3. Defense Against Intruders. Secure Wi-Fi networks prevent unauthorized users from gaining access to your network, reducing the risk of cyberattacks and data theft.

Key Steps to Set Up a Secure Wi-Fi Network

1. Change the Default Credentials. The first and most critical step is to change the default username and password for your Wi-Fi router. Default credentials are well-known to attackers and should be replaced with strong, unique combinations.

2. Enable WPA3 Encryption. Use the latest Wi-Fi encryption protocol, WPA3, to secure your network. WPA3 provides robust encryption, making it significantly harder for unauthorized users to access your network.

3. Hide Your Network Name (SSID). Consider hiding your network's SSID, making it less visible to potential attackers. While this doesn't provide absolute security, it adds an extra layer of protection.

4. Implement a Strong Password. Set a strong, unique password for your Wi-Fi network. Avoid using easily guessable passwords, and consider using a passphrase.

5. Enable a Firewall. Activate the firewall on your router to filter incoming and outgoing traffic, blocking potentially harmful data packets.

6. Regularly Update Router Firmware. Keep your router's firmware up to date. Updates often include security patches to address vulnerabilities.

7. Use MAC Address Filtering. Implement MAC address filtering to only allow specific devices to connect to your network. While not foolproof, it adds an extra layer of security.

8. Regularly Check Connected Devices. Periodically review the devices connected to your network. Disconnect any unknown or unauthorized devices.

9. Consider a Separate Guest Network. If your router allows it, set up a separate guest network to isolate guest traffic from your primary network.

10. Educate Family Members. Ensure that family members using the network know security practices and follow guidelines for safe online behavior.

By taking these steps, you can establish a secure Wi-Fi network that is the foundation for defending your digital starship. It's your first line of defense in the digital cosmos, protecting your online identity and activities from unwanted intrusions and threats.

5.3. Being a Responsible Guardian in the Digital Galaxy

As we traverse the ever-expanding digital galaxy, we take on the role of responsible guardians not only for our online presence but also for the safety and well-being of the broader digital community. The digital cosmos is a vast, interconnected realm where our actions and choices impact not only our lives but also those of countless others. Being a responsible guardian in this space is not only a matter of self-preservation but a duty to protect and foster a safe and thriving digital environment.

The Responsibilities of a Digital Guardian

1. Cyber Hygiene. Responsible guardians practice good "cyber hygiene" by following best practices for online security. This includes using strong passwords, keeping software up to date, and being vigilant against cyber threats.

2. Privacy Advocacy. Guardians are advocates for digital privacy. They understand the importance of personal privacy and advocate for policies and practices that protect individuals' data and online rights.

3. Educating Others. Responsible guardians share their knowledge with friends, family, and colleagues. They educate others about online safety, security, and reliable digital citizenship.

4. Promoting Digital Literacy. Guardians work to enhance digital literacy, helping people become more discerning consumers of online content and more capable digital citizens.

5. Online Etiquette. Being courteous and respectful in online interactions is another aspect of digital responsibility. Responsible guardians foster a culture of positive online behavior.

6. Supporting Digital Inclusion. They advocate for digital inclusion, recognizing that access to the digital cosmos is a fundamental right. Efforts are made to bridge the digital divide and ensure that everyone can participate in the digital world.

Protection of Vulnerable Individuals

Responsible guardians also recognize the vulnerabilities of some individuals in the digital realm. Children, the elderly, and those with limited digital experience may be more susceptible to online threats. Guardians take extra care to protect these individuals and provide guidance as needed.

Stewardship of Digital Spaces

Digital guardians take on the role of stewards of the digital spaces they inhabit. They participate in preserving these spaces, whether by reporting abusive content, volunteering in online communities, or advocating for a safe and inclusive digital environment.

Responsible Guardianship in Action

By actively engaging in responsible guardianship in the digital galaxy, we collectively create a safer and more prosperous digital realm. As responsible guardians, we navigate the digital cosmos not only for our benefit but with the understanding that our actions have a broader impact. Just as explorers of old sought to preserve the natural environment, we strive to safeguard the digital environment for future generations.

In conclusion, being a responsible guardian in the digital galaxy is a multifaceted role that combines personal online security with a commitment to the well-being of the digital community. By taking on this role with diligence and dedication, we can ensure that the digital cosmos remains a place of exploration, innovation, and connection while being safe and secure for all who journey through it.

GLOSSARY

Antivirus Software. Software designed to detect, prevent, and remove malicious software (malware) from devices.

Biometrics. Security measures that use unique physical or behavioral characteristics, such as fingerprints or facial recognition, for authentication.

Cyber Threats. Potential dangers in the digital realm, such as cyberattacks, malware, and data breaches.

Cybersecurity. The practice of protecting computer systems, networks, and data from theft, damage, or unauthorized access.

Data Breach. Unauthorized access to sensitive information, resulting in its exposure or theft.

Digital Galaxy. A metaphorical term referring to the vast and interconnected digital world, including the internet, devices, and online services.

Digital Identity. The online representation of an individual, including personal information, login credentials, and digital activities.

Digital Inclusion. The effort to ensure that everyone has access to and can participate in the digital world.

Digital Starship. A metaphorical term referring to an individual's devices and online presence in the digital cosmos.

Firewall. A security system that monitors and controls incoming and outgoing network traffic based on predetermined security rules.

Identity Theft. The act of stealing personal information to assume someone else's identity for fraudulent purposes.

Malware. A broad category of malicious software, including viruses, Trojans, spyware, and ransomware, can harm devices and steal data.

Online Etiquette. Following courteous and respectful behavior in online interactions.

Online Fraud. Deceptive schemes or scams that aim to defraud individuals or organizations online, including investment fraud and shopping scams.

Phishing Attacks. Cybercriminals use deceptive tactics to trick individuals into revealing sensitive information, often through fraudulent emails, messages, or websites.

Responsible Guardian of the Galaxy. A metaphorical term referring to an individual who takes an active role in protecting their digital presence and the online safety of others.

Two-Factor Authentication (2FA). A security measure that requires users to provide two different authentication factors to access an account or system.

Wi-Fi Network. A wireless network that connects devices to the internet or a local network.

INDEX

BIBLIOGRAPHY

- Auger, G., Scott, J. "., Helmus, J., Nguyen, K., & Heath "The Cyber Mentor" Adams. (2021). Cybersecurity career master plan: Proven techniques and effective tips to help you advance in your cybersecurity career. Packt Publishing.
- Grubb, S. (2021). How cybersecurity really works: A hands-on guide for total beginners. No Starch Press.
- Kleymenov, A., & Thabet, A. (2019). Mastering malware analysis: The complete malware analyst's guide to combating malicious software, APT, cybercrime, and IoT attacks. Packt Publishing.
- Lee, N. (2015). Counterterrorism and cybersecurity: Total information awareness. Springer.
- Pelton, J., & Singh, I. B. (2015). Digital defense: A cybersecurity primer. Springer.
- Schuette, S. L. (2019). undefined. Pebble.
- Teens, J. (2018). Cyber safety for everyone: Online risks can be dangerous stay informed. BPB Publications.
- Vasiliu-Feltes, I., & Thomason, J. (2021). Applied ethics in a digital world. IGI Global.

About the Book

"Guardians of the Digital Galaxy: Cybersecurity for Beginners" is your guide to navigating the ever-expansive digital universe with confidence and security. As our lives become increasingly entwined with the digital cosmos, this book empowers you to be the vigilant protector of your digital starship. With the knowledge, skills, and insights shared within these pages, you will embark on a journey to understand and thwart cyber threats, safeguard your online identity, and explore the profound importance of cybersecurity. Whether you are a newcomer to the digital realm or seeking to bolster your online safety practices, this book serves as your steadfast companion, offering a roadmap to a secure digital voyage and a means to become a true Guardian of the Digital Galaxy.

About the Author

Kevin D. Caratiquit is a Senior High School Teacher III at Lal-lo National High School, where he specializes in ICT, research, and statistics. His dedication centers on shaping young minds, fostering academic excellence, and kindling a love for learning. With a Doctor of Philosophy in Education majoring in Educational Management, a Master of Science in Information Technology from Cagayan State University Aparri, and a Bachelor of Science in Computer Science from Lyceum of Aparri, he exhibits an unwavering commitment to personal and scholarly growth. As School Research , and ICT Coordinator, he actively contributes to educational advancement, and his international research articles in reputable journals underscore his dedication to academic progress. His multifaceted role in education aligns seamlessly with the invaluable insights he provides in **"Guardians of the Digital Galaxy: Cybersecurity for Beginners."**

Published by

Poetry Planet Book Publishing House

Call or Text: 09554960044
Email: maritesritumalta@gmail.com |
lovelypoetess95@gmail.com
Website: https://poetryplanet114433.wixsite.com/website-1

Registered with and Accredited by
the National Book Development Board of the Philippines

www.ingramcontent.com/pod-product-compliance
Lightning Source LLC
LaVergne TN
LVHW010503160826
845677LV00012B/2627

* 9 7 8 6 2 1 4 7 0 9 9 2 2 *